thi

belongs

t

D0284187

Alberto Corral, a native of the Canary Islands, Spain, lived in many cities around the world before hanging his hat in Los Angeles, California. He currently works as a character animator for DreamWorks Animation.

A man of many talents, Alberto doesn't just write children's books; he is also a filmmaker and screenwriter. His passion is for storytelling in any form. He enjoys life in sunny California with his lovely wife, Carolina, scouting the city for the perfect dessert (he is very close).

Alessandra Sorrentino lives in Turin, Italy. She was raised on pasta and Japanese anime. She now works as an animator, a story artist, and an illustrator for Cartoon Network, Disney, and BBC. She loves cats, cooking, and vintage typewriters.

My
Monster
Burrufu

Alberto Corral

illustrated by Alessandra Sorrentino

PETITE GRANDE IDÉE

First published in 2011
by Petite Grande Idée
Los Angeles, California

Translated by Carolina Lorén

Printed in the United States of America

ISBN-10: 061545934X
ISBN-13: 978-0615459349

Library of Congress Control Number
2011904846

To Carolina—

my wife and my best friend,
who always believed in me,
even when I didn't believe in myself.

CONTENTS

My
Monster
Burrufu

My name is Olivia Norby. My dad is the writer Steven Norby. I am seven years old. Today is a big day for us. It is moving day. Today we leave the big city to go live in a very big house in the country. So, please take good care of the house we're leaving you. I will really miss it. Hugs and kisses to the new tenant.

Sincerely,
Olivia

1. A New House

"Let's go, Olivia!" her father yelled.

"I'm coming!" she answered, sealing her note in an envelope and dropping it on a table.

Olivia was a very sharp and silly girl. She always wore dresses and flat shoes. She had coal-black hair. Maybe it was a little short compared to the other girls in her class, but it went down to her shoulders, and she held it up with two pigtails.

Olivia could hardly stand still. She always ran from one end of the house to the other. And she always had a smile that brightened her whole face.

"Let's go, Tula," she said, hurrying up her dog. Tula was small and white, with very long ears and very short legs. Her father had surprised her with the dog on her birthday a few years ago so that she would have someone to play with.

"Come on, Olivia. Mark's waiting downstairs."

Mark was Steve's editor. He was a kind and grateful person and always well dressed. He had one tiny fault, if you could even call it that. He was always looking to take advantage of everything. It was not that he was a bad person and wanted to take advantage of people— not in the least. He simply really liked money.

Steve had called Mark to help him move because they had been friends since they were children, and now they were business partners. Besides, Mark had a van, which always comes in handy when you have to move.

Steve was a writer who'd achieved a certain level of success. His professional career was just about to take off.

All of his work was finally starting to pay off. His look was a bit bohemian, which clashed with Mark's elegance, but that is what friendships are about. Every person is who they are, and we must learn to accept it.

"Hello, Mark!" Olivia greeted him excitedly as she got into the van.

"Hello, honey," replied Mark. "Let's go! Let's go! It will be dark soon."

"You're exaggerating." Olivia giggled. "It's nine in the morning, and Dad said it will take about four hours. We'll get there at...at..."

"I'll tell you if you give me a dollar bill."

"Hey!" interrupted Olivia's father. "Have some respect. You're trying to steal from my daughter." He turned toward Olivia. "Don't listen to him, darling. If you give me the dollar, I will tell you."

"Hey, that's cheating!" exclaimed Mark.

Olivia laughed while the adults argued about who was supposed to get paid.

Then their grand journey began. They passed through the city. It was a small city, full of stores and people sipping coffee in outdoor cafés. People walked around in their elegant dresses and Borsalino hats. The roads were made of cobblestones. Olivia greeted everyone she saw, and they always greeted her back.

After a few hours in the van, they finally arrived at Steve and Olivia's new home. It hadn't been such a long trip after all, but to Olivia it had seemed an eternity. She was used to everything being so close in the city, and when anything took more than half an hour to reach, it seemed to her like it was very, very far away.

Olivia jumped out of the van. Before her was a huge old house, three stories tall and full of windows. It looked like a house from a horror movie. It was made of antique wood, but you could no longer make out its color. It was black, or perhaps it was brown and had darkened over time.

They had decided to move there—actually, her dad had decided to do so—because it was away from the noise of the city. This way Steve could write peacefully. Besides, it was cheaper.

"What do you think?" Steve asked his daughter.

Olivia's face lit up. Her eyes looked around the entire house. "I love it!" she shouted, full of joy. Then she hesitated. "But it does scare me a little."

"Don't worry," Steve reassured her. "You'll change your mind when you see your room."

Olivia smiled when she heard those words and took off running to see her new room, Tula ran barking behind her. Olivia threw open the front door.

WHAM!

Everything was silent. Olivia was still for a second, looking around everywhere.

There was a lot of space for her to run and play. While her father and Mark unloaded the bags and moving boxes, Olivia slipped away to explore all the nooks and crannies of the new house.

She went all over the floors in just a few seconds. She went up the stairs and down the stairs. She opened the door to one room, then another.

The house was full of hallways. It looked like a maze. But that didn't make any difference to Olivia. She was becoming more and more excited with each new place she discovered... until she heard a strange noise coming from overhead.

Olivia stopped and looked at the ceiling. "Shhh...quiet, Tula," she said in a low voice.

Something had moved up there. Olivia slowly pushed a chair to the wall and climbed on top of it. She quietly reached as high as she could on the wall and placed her ear against it. Suddenly, an enormous bang rang out and scared her so much she fell off the chair.

She yelled and ran in search of her father, who was setting up his typewriter in his office. "Daddy, Daddy!" Olivia said, terrified. "I heard something. There is something moving above us."

"That's impossible, sweetheart. There aren't any other floors above us. We're already on the third floor." Her father tried to make her feel better. "This is an old house. Perhaps it was the wind," he went on while he organized his things. "Or perhaps..." He paused and stared right at Olivia.

"What? What?!" exclaimed Olivia.

"Or perhaps it is a monster!" her father shouted, making funny faces and pretending he was a big bear.

Olivia quickly realized that her father was making fun of her. "It isn't funny, Dad. I'm being serious."

Steve laughed when he saw his daughter with her arms crossed, looking so serious. "There isn't anything to be worried about. Monsters are a sign of good luck. If you have a monster at home, it means you will have good luck."

Olivia was angry. "You're always making fun of me."

She would have never admitted it, but that answer—although she was angry at her dad because of the way he had frightened her—relieved her a lot. Knowing that monsters brought good luck is always a relief.

2. The Encounter

It was midnight. The day had been exhausting for everyone. Steve was already asleep, although he still had his clothes on. He had the sheets twisted around him and between his legs. He was so tired he'd probably stay asleep even if the roof fell down on him.

Olivia was in her room tossing and turning in her bed. She was trying to sleep, but something was going 'round and 'round in her head. She closed her eyes tight, but she couldn't sleep.

Is there a monster? What's he like? Does he want to be my friend? she thought.

"I wish he wanted to be my friend," she murmured.

After a while of tossing and turning in her bed, Olivia got up. She put on her little shoes with the mouse faces on them and walked to her father's room. He was deeply asleep. She softly tugged on his sleeve, trying to wake him up.

"Dad," she whispered. "Daddy...Dad?...DAD!"

"WHAT!" Steve exclaimed, startled. "Ah, it's you, Olivia. What's wrong, honey?"

"I can't sleep. Can I have milk and cookies?"

"Mmmkay, but go to bed immmmediately...no TVzzz," he said as he moved back to his favorite sleeping position.

"Okay!" Olivia smiled. "Come on, Tula!"

"Shhh!" he silenced her.

"I mean, come on, Tula."

Olivia walked down to the kitchen and turned on only one light. She grabbed a big glass from the sink. She was so small that it was hard for her to get to the countertop, but she could do it by opening the bottom drawer of a cabinet and hopping inside. Her father wouldn't approve, but now he was asleep, so how would he know? She grabbed milk from the fridge and a plate of cookies and sat on a stool at the kitchen table. Tula, who was still sleepy, yawned and waited for a piece of cookie.

Olivia was eating absentmindedly, swinging her feet and looking at her new kitchen, which was hard to see in the dark. In fact, only the table was lighted. But even so, she looked around the room and felt really excited. She hardly looked at her glass and plate. Her head swung from side to side.

After a couple of cookies, Olivia finished her glass of milk in one gulp. She jumped off the stool, stretched her arms, and switched off the kitchen light. She started walking back to her room. Halfway up the stairs, she realized that she forgot to put the milk inside the fridge. She didn't feel like going back, but her father would be mad in the morning if he found the milk on the counter. So she turned around and started down the stairs.

Suddenly, Tula bared her teeth and started to growl. She only did that with people she didn't know. She bolted down the stairs, barking.

milk

"Tula! Quiet! It's not time to bark!" Olivia shouted, chasing Tula.

Olivia burst into the kitchen and hit the light. And there it was.

The monster.

Olivia smiled. "I knew it," she whispered to herself.

With so little light, she could see only one big hand—furry and white, with sharp gray nails—grabbing a few cookies off the plate she had left. In the dark, she could make out a bigger figure, larger than a bear, larger than anything Olivia had seen before.

All three stood, frozen. Tula stopped barking. Olivia kept smiling. The monster didn't move an inch.

Suddenly, the monster turned and ran with several cookies clutched in his hand. Olivia and Tula chased after him. They ran through the dark. Olivia couldn't see much, just glimpses of shadows. But she heard perfectly his giant footsteps.

He's so big! she thought.

He ran through the whole house, trailing pieces of cookies through the hallways and on the stairs.

"Wait!" Olivia yelled.

The chase didn't last long. Olivia turned a corner and ran straight into a dead end. There was only a wall and two closed windows.

"It's gone," she said, amazed. The only clue was the pile of broken cookies on the floor.

Quickly she went to warn her father. Olivia was so excited! How could she not be?

"Dad, Dad! I've seen it!" she said, waking him up abruptly.

"What the...? What? How?" he asked, startled by the loud awakening.

"The monster. Dad, you were right."

"Monster? What monster?"

"The lucky charm monster! He lives with us."

"Ooookay." Steve cradled Olivia, tucking her into bed with him. "Weeee'll talk about it tomorrowzzz," he mumbled, half asleep. "Now sleep."

"But Dad...!"

"Shhh."

Olivia couldn't sleep. It was impossible. She was excited. Enthusiastic.

Olivia looked up at the ceiling. "Thanks," she whispered. She finally closed her eyes and slept, with a big smile on her face the whole night.

3. The Trap

The next morning, very early, Olivia was having breakfast with her father. She was still so excited, she couldn't stop talking. She talked about how the monster looked, how it moved, what it ate. And, of course, she exaggerated everything.

Steve smiled as much as he could for how sleepy he felt. "I'mmm happy that you...have a nnneeew friend," he yawned. "Just tell me one thing, Olivia. Why is the house filled with cookies?"

"It's the monster, Dad. He eats cookies."

Olivia kept talking nonstop while her father filled his mug with more coffee. Without his morning coffee, it was impossible for him to wake up.

"Why don't you take a picture of him the next time?" asked Steve.

"I don't know where he is," said Olivia thoughtfully. "He just disappeared."

"Ohhhhh, a monster with powers...fascinating." Her father pulled a face like he was really interested.

"I didn't say he had powers. I only said he disappeared."

"Of course, of course," he answered in a humoring voice.

The phone rang, interrupting the conversation. Olivia rushed to pick it up. She loved answering the phone.

"Hello, who's calling?" She paused. "Okay. Dad, it's Mark!"

Steve was still wearing his pajama pants and an old T-shirt, his eyes still full of sleep. He didn't feel like talking on the phone. "Why are you calling me so early in the morning?" he asked into the phone. "I already told you I'll bring the rough draft tomorrow."

His face changed from sleepy to fully alert in a millisecond. "What? Was it today?" Panicked, he looked at his watch. "Okay, okay! I'm going!"

"OLIVIA!" he called, as if she were upstairs.

"Yes?" she answered. She was just beside him, and he hadn't noticed. He still needed that extra coffee.

"I have to leave for the TV interview," he said running from one side of the house to the other, grabbing papers, looking for his suitcase, his jacket....

"I totally forgot about it. Remember, be good. I'll be back soon. Don't forget to set the DVR. I want to see myself."

"Don't worry, Dad." Olivia said to calm him down.

"Remember, if something happens, call me, whatever it is, and don't open the door to anyone." He kissed her and said good-bye at the door, then continued giving orders while hopping to the car. He was still calling out instructions as the car pulled away.

"Be good! I'll be back soon! I love you! Clean your rooooom....." Olivia watched her father's car disappear down the road, while his voice faded in the distance. Then, smiling, she ran into the house and slammed the door.

She grabbed a camera from a drawer and placed several cookies on the floor right where the monster had disappeared. She pushed the hallway table over so she could hop on it later and have a better shooting angle. She had everything prepared.

Olivia started walking away, stomping loudly with each step. *BAM! BAM! BAM!*

"This is so boooring! I think I'm going to play outside!" she shouted, pretending to go out. She opened the front door and, without going out, closed it so loudly it could be heard throughout the whole house.

BAM!

And so it was. The slam was heard on every floor. Afterward, carefully, quietly, she crept upstairs on her tiptoes and jumped on top of the hallway table she had previously moved. The cookies were still there. Good. Her plan felt perfect.

She waited and waited, but nothing happened. She kept waiting and waiting, and still nothing happened.

The silence and the boredom almost made Olivia fall asleep on her feet with the camera in her hands— until Tula barked and broke the monotony.

Olivia jumped at the noise but recovered quickly. "Shhhhh! Quiet, Tula," Olivia whispered. "You're going to frighten him away."

But Tula wouldn't stop barking. She needed to go to the backyard to answer nature's call. Olivia didn't know what to do. If she left her spot, she could miss the monster. But if she stayed there, Tula would pee on the floor and Olivia would have to clean it up afterward.

"Come on, let's go." She jumped off the table and ran to open the back door. Quickly she returned to her surveillance spot. But sadly for her, all the cookies were gone. Olivia couldn't believe it. Only a few crumbs were left on the floor.

She looked everywhere: the windows, the floors, the ceiling. It didn't make any sense. She jumped on top of the hallway table again. Maybe from there she could get a better idea of what had just happened. She was looking and looking everywhere, nervous and disappointed. She was leaning so much to look that the little table became unbalanced and tipped over. She was about to fall, but she was able to grab on to a wall lamp. Under her weight, the lamp bent and a secret door in the wall swung open.

Olivia looked at the opening, bewildered. She got down from the lamp with care and slowly approached the door. She opened it wide and discovered stairs leading up, apparently to an attic, a place she and her father hadn't known existed. It was hidden between the top floor and the roof.

Olivia moved closer. She was trying to find out what was there, but it was very dark. There was only a small light at the top of the stairs. And from somewhere up there she could hear a mix of growling and someone— or something—chewing.

Olivia was overwhelmed. Her body filled with nerves and anxiety, happiness and fear. She carefully put one foot on the first step, but suddenly realized that she needed protection. Just in case.

She knew that monsters were a blessing for good luck. That's what her father had told her. But she didn't know if the monster that lived upstairs was also friendly. Her father hadn't told her about friendship with monsters.

Olivia went down the stairs quietly and ran into the kitchen, where she searched through drawers and cabinets. After a while she appeared in front of the secret door covered in armor made of casserole dishes, pans, lids, and wooden spoons.

Half the kitchen was taped to her little body, protecting her like a medieval knight. She wore a metal colander on her head. Spoons hung from her waist like swords.

She took a deep breath, calming down as much as she could. Then she started going up, step by step, without making the smallest noise.

After a few steps, she started to see something at the end of the attic. It looked like a big and furry monster, but she could only see him from behind. He wore a yellow-and-red striped scarf around his hairy neck. By his movements, Olivia guessed that he was eating the cookies she had put out as bait.

Her eyes opened wide in admiration. What a big, chubby monster! Even though his hands had large nails and, once in a while, she could see glimpses of fangs in his mouth, Olivia wasn't afraid. Well, she might have been a little bit, but the excitement of having a monster in her home made her overcome the little fear she had.

Olivia moved stealthily, walking on her tiptoes. She lifted her camera and took a picture, but as luck would have it, her flash was set on automatic.

The flash scared the monster, and he screamed. That made Olivia scream too, and she stumbled and hurt her elbow. Then she started to cry.

The monster started to grow bigger and bigger. He tried to hide behind some boxes and papers, but he got so big that Olivia could see him perfectly.

"Shhh, shhh. Please, don't be scared," said the monster, nervously, from his hiding spot. "Calm down, please.... Please...don't cry."

Olivia was astonished. The monster could *talk*. She wiped her tears with her hand and went from tears to a smile in only a few seconds.

"H-Hello?" she whispered in a very sweet voice.

Nobody answered. Olivia moved a few steps closer to see the hiding monster.

"Hello?" she repeated.

The monster still didn't answer and was trying to hide himself even more. Olivia moved some boxes and papers away, letting his face show. No one said a word. Silence filled the room.

The monster didn't want to look at her. Whenever their eyes met, the monster looked in the other direction. His face was filled with worry, but Olivia's was filled with happiness. Olivia went around the boxes and stepped right in front of him. He didn't know where to hide. Behind him there were more boxes that blocked the only possible exit, and in front of him was a fascinated Olivia.

She couldn't wait any longer and jumped toward the monster. He seemed so soft that she just wanted to hug and pet him. Olivia held tight to his belly.

The monster stood up, stiff and scared.

He didn't expect that kind of reaction. Suddenly, the monster started shrinking smaller and smaller, back to his regular size, which was still pretty big.

With that sudden change, Olivia slipped and almost fell down, but quickly the monster grabbed her by the leg, letting only her armor touch the ground, not her. And again there was silence. They looked at each other for a few seconds without saying a word.

The monster kept holding her by the leg when Olivia, who was upside down, broke the silence. "HI!"

The monster didn't answer. He seemed more surprised about her than she was about him.

"What's your name?" Olivia asked.

After a few more seconds, the monster finally opened his mouth. "Bu-Bu-Burrufu," he stuttered.

Olivia smiled. "BURRUFU! I love it!"

Burrufu still didn't know what to do.

"Thanks a lot for living in this house and giving us good luck," Olivia said.

Burrufu stared at her, even more confused than ever.

"Can you let me down?" Olivia asked softly. "I'm getting dizzy. All the blood is going to my head."

Burrufu flipped her over and put her down delicately. Once she was on the floor and fully recovered from being upside down, Burrufu made a gesture for her to go, like he was shooing away an unknown dog.

Olivia took no notice of it and started looking all around the attic. She was amazed! There were mountains of paper—thousands of books, single sheets of paper in one place, other pieces of paper stapled together. They came in every kind and color. Well, basically there were two colors—white and old yellow—but in those two colors, there were many variations.

Olivia started touching and picking up everything in sight. Every single thing she grabbed, Burrufu went after her, took it from her hands, and put it back in its place.

"Amazing," she said. "All of this is awesome."

"Okay," Burrufu answered, "I think it's time for you to go."

Olivia kept staring like she hadn't heard Burrufu at all. How was she going to go? It was an attic with a monster! She was too excited.

On the table was an old typewriter with a sheet of paper in it and a stack of written paper by its side. Olivia approached the table to look at it.

She quickly realized that those were not just any papers. They were a manuscript, the original work of an author. They were books that had never been published. She recognized them very easily because she had already seen lots of them in her father's office. In that moment, Olivia realized that Burrufu was a writer.

"Are you a writer?" she happily exclaimed. "Like my fath—"

"Yes, yes, that's wonderful. Now go," Burrufu interrupted.

Burrufu was pushing her to leave. He didn't want to know anything about her. He didn't want to make any contact with anyone. But he was also just a little curious, because even though he wanted to kick her out, he was amazed that she wasn't scared of him, that she wanted to be there...with him.

But, he thought, *it's better if she leaves.*

"Again, thanks for the good luck," said Olivia.

"What good luck?" he asked, surprised, still pushing her toward the stairs.

"You know, having a monster at home is a sign of good luck. My dad told me."

"Your father! Does he know I'm here?"

"No," she answered, "but wait until I tell him. He's going to love you. He's also a writer, you know."

"You know what? It's better if you don't tell him, okay?" Burrufu insisted nervously. "We'll keep it a—"

"A secret?" Olivia happily exclaimed.

"Yes, that, perfect. We'll keep it a secret. It will be *our* secret."

"Okay! But only if I can come visit you."

Burrufu was stuck between a rock and a hard place. Olivia had dodged his last attempt to keep her away.

"Okay," he said, resigned, "but only if you leave now."

"Great!" Olivia hugged him, but Burrufu did everything he could to avoid any contact. She started to go down the stairs, and Burrufu sighed in relief and despair.

"Hey!" Olivia said, sticking her head back through the door. "Tomorrow I'll bring you more cookies."

Right at the moment Olivia was closing the secret entrance, she heard her father coming in through the front door. She quickly ran to the kitchen, jumped on to a stool, and put a cookie in her mouth to disguise anything unusual.

Steve entered the kitchen and, of course, found Olivia eating cookies "How are you, sweetie?"

"Mmmoookay," she said with her mouth full.

"By the way, where's Tula? It's weird she didn't come say hi."

"Tula!" Olivia ran to open the back door so Tula could come in. With everything that had happened, she had completely forgotten about her dog.

When she returned, her dad was reading the newspaper on the couch. "So, did you record my interview?"

"Oh! I forgot. I'm sorry."

"Well, I just hope Mark recorded it. So, what did you do all day, sweetie? Did you get a picture of the monster?"

"MONSTER? WHAT MONSTER?!" Olivia yelled in a very loud and dramatic voice. **"THERE'S NO MONSTER!"**

"That's a shame," Steve answered, "because a monster at home is always good news."

Olivia climbed up the armrest and made a gesture to her father to come closer. When she had his ear next to her mouth, she whispered, "His name is Burrufu and he loves cookies, but it's a secret."

Her father winked. "Of course, sweetie, of course."

Then he sighed heavily. He suddenly got up, stretched his arms, folded the newspaper, and went to his office to work. And, like always, with the habit of yelling things while he walked away, he said, "By the way, this Wednesday the people from the network are coming here to record an interview. We have to make sure the house is clean!"

4. I Love Your Book

Very early the next day, Olivia went to the attic with Tula in her arms. She wanted her dog to meet Burrufu, who she found very focused on writing one of his novels.

"Hello!" she yelled. "I want to introduce you to Tula."

Burrufu sighed when he saw his visitors. It was crystal clear he wasn't happy having her around. But what could he do? That was the deal they made.

Burrufu enjoyed his solitude, his calmness. He didn't like to have contact with anyone. He only liked himself and his old typewriter.

"What are you doing?" asked Olivia as she released Tula so the little dog could stretch her legs.

"I'm working," Burrufu answered, very serious.

"Hey," Olivia continued, "why are you a monster? How old are you? What do you eat? And...and...and...where do you come from?"

Burrufu interrupted her, putting his palm to her face. When she was quiet, he made the silence sign with his finger against his lips. "Shhhhhhh..."

Olivia kept quiet, looking intensely at his finger.

Burrufu remained silent. He sighed again, took a breath, closed his eyes, and focused again on his work. Once he was on track, he put his little glasses on and kept writing. The only sound came from the keys of the typewriter.

It *was* the only sound...until Olivia opened her mouth again. "What are you writing? Can I read it? Am I in your book?"

"Shhh!" Burrufu interrupted again.

Olivia stared at him without saying a word. After a few moments of silence, she spoke again. "Don't you get bored of being alone?"

Burrufu grumbled. The girl got on his nerves. "Aaaarggghhhh! It's over. I can't stand it anymore. You're going to make me mad, and then I'll have to scare you."

"That's impossible!" Olivia laughed. "How are you going to scare me if you are super cute?"

"Are you sure?"

"Yep."

"If I scare you, will you leave?" asked Burrufu with hope.

"Okay," answered Olivia, very excited.

Burrufu got up, cleared his throat, took a deep breath, and started to roar, opening his mouth as wide as he could and showing all his teeth. A big blast of air lifted everything in the room. Tula was so scared that she ran to hide behind Olivia's legs.

Olivia stood in front of Burrufu, quietly, looking at him with wide eyes and an astonished face. When he had used up all the air in his lungs, Olivia happily jumped and wrapped her arms around his belly.

"You are so cute!" she exclaimed.

Burrufu couldn't believe it. He sighed again in despair. "Listen, don't you have another place where you can annoy someone?" he asked tiredly, peeling her off and putting her on the ground.

Olivia picked up Tula to calm her down and shook her head.

Burrufu stared at her. "Okay, if you stay quiet for a while, I'll play with you later or whatever it is that you do. But only if you don't bother me now."

Olivia happily accepted his offer. Burrufu sat down and returned to his typewriter.

Soon Olivia and Tula started running around the attic. Burrufu was trying to concentrate, but he was getting distracted by every step and laugh coming from the two visitors. He breathed deeply, trying to calm down.

Olivia and Tula kept running.

Burrufu breathed. They ran. Breathed, ran, breathed, ran, breathed, breathed, breathed...until he couldn't stand it any longer!

"ENOUGH! Get out! That's enough! Get out of here!" he screamed.

"Why? We didn't talk!" Olivia defended herself as Burrufu pushed her toward the stairs.

"Come on, get out," he insisted.

"Okay, I'll leave, but under one condition."

"What?"

"Do the same trick you did yesterday, when you grew and shrank."

"What?"

"Yes, what you did yesterday, when you got big, then returned to your normal size."

Burrufu's face changed. That comment made him feel sad and serious. "That...wasn't...a trick."

"Ah, it wasn't? So what was it?"

"It was nothing. Leave it. Please leave." Burrufu stopped pushing her and returned to his small chair. He slowly sat down at his desk, but he didn't start working. He simply looked into the distance with his head low. Burrufu turned his back to Olivia.

Olivia saw how his mood had changed. She understood that she shouldn't be there, that this was not the time, so she left without even saying good-bye.

Right before going downstairs, Olivia stumbled over the kitchen utensils she had used as armor the day before. Without paying any attention, and still looking at Burrufu, she picked up everything that was on the floor.

Olivia walked as well as she could. She had so many things in her arms that she could barely see the stairs. She went right into the kitchen to put away all the things she had taken for protection. Wooden spoons, lid covers, a metal colander...a book?

She realized she had one of Burrufu's manuscripts. She thought about returning it, but in that same moment she heard her father getting closer. So she ran to her room, threw the book under her bed, and went back to the kitchen like nothing had happened.

That night, Olivia climbed into bed and waited for her father to tuck her in. "Good night, Dad," she said as he kissed her good night.

"Should I turn off the light?"

"No, I want to read a little."

"What do you want to read tonight?"

Olivia started to think. She had the habit of biting her lower lip when she was thinking. "Ehhh...that one", she said, pointing at the bookcase.

Steve walked over to the shelf. "Which one? This?"

"Yes, that one," Olivia answered quickly.

"All right, here it is, but don't stay up late reading."

"Okay!"

"Good night, honey."

When her father left and Olivia was sure that he wasn't nearby, she threw the book to the floor and looked under her bed. Burrufu's manuscript was still there. Excited, Olivia started to read it in the light of her small lamp.

The next morning Olivia was having breakfast with her father, who was buried in the newspaper, as usual, doing a crossword. Olivia was eating cookies and looking at the ceiling as she swung her feet.

"Any plans for today, honey?" her father asked without raising his head. He was still doing his crossword.

"Mmmmm...nope," she answered with her mouth full. "I don't know. Maybe I'll paint a little, and then I'll go play outside with Tula."

"That sounds like a plan." He was still focused on the words.

Suddenly, he stretched his arms, drank the rest of his coffee in one gulp, and stood up. He was a man who could go from asleep to totally alert in just a few seconds.

"It's time to go to work," he said and kissed Olivia on the top her head.

When he was gone, Olivia got down off the chair and made sure her father was on his way to his office. She quickly cleaned her breakfast from the table, put her mug in the sink, took a plastic bag from a drawer, filled it with chocolate cookies and put it in her backpack.

"Dad, I've changed my mind. I'm going to play outside!" she yelled from the kitchen.

"Okay! Be careful!" he called back from his office.

Olivia opened the back door and closed it with a slam, but she stayed inside the house. Then, on her tiptoes but without losing any time, Olivia headed to the hallway, triggered the lamp, and went up the attic.

Burrufu was, as always, focused on writing. Tula ran toward him, full of happiness, and jumped into his lap. She only growled at the people she didn't know, and Burrufu was no longer a stranger.

"Hi, Burrufu," said Olivia happily.

Burrufu looked to the ceiling and grumbled. He didn't like Olivia and Tula bothering him. Burrufu was rough, and he didn't know how to treat people nicely. He enjoyed his loneliness. He liked silence. For him, living in a lonely world was perfect...although he may have been living alone for too long, which is never a good thing.

Olivia got closer to the table. "What are you doing?" she asked.

"Working," he answered, very serious. "Why don't you go play outside? Don't you have any friends to play with?" He hoped that she would leave.

"No. The kids from my class say I'm weird."

Burrufu wasn't surprised by that.

"But I don't care what they say," she continued. "I don't need them. I have Tula, and now I have you."

"Is that what I am to you?" asked Burrufu, angry. He took off his reading glasses. "Some kind of pet?"

"No, no, no," Olivia quickly interrupted. "I meant a friend. Tula is my friend, and I thought that you might want to be our friend."

"I don't want to be your friend," he said sharply and returned to his typing machine.

Olivia only listened to the things she was interested in, so obviously, that kind of comment went unnoticed. "By the way," she continued, "I loved your book."

Burrufu quickly turned to look at her. "What book?"

"This one." She took out the manuscript from her backpack.

Burrufu snatched it from her hands. "WHO GAVE YOU THE RIGHT TO TAKE MY THINGS?!" he yelled. He was very angry.

"I-I-I'm sorry," Olivia stuttered anxiously. "I didn't mean to take it. It was thrown on the—"

Outraged, Burrufu stood up. "Didn't your mother teach you not to take things without permission?"

"I didn't...know my mom," she replied sadly.

"THAT IS NOT AN EXCUSE TO TOUCH MY THINGS!" he screamed again, so angry he was shaking.

Burrufu quieted down, though he was still grumbling. He turned. He didn't want to look at her. He realized that he shouldn't have made that comment. Maybe his solitude had made him forget how to treat a kid. Too much alone time was never good.

Olivia stood looking at him sadly. Tula was hiding between her legs.

Burrufu looked at Olivia and saw tears filling her eyes. "I'm sorry about your mother, okay?" he said sharply.

Olivia couldn't help it any longer and burst into tears. "Maybe you should learn not to take cookies that aren't yours!" Olivia shouted as she ran away.

Burrufu didn't know what to do or how to answer. He felt terrible for yelling at her about taking other people's things when he did the same thing himself.

"Bah, I don't care," he said to himself. "At least she'll learn not to touch what's not hers."

As he went to put the book in its place, a paper fell out from inside the pages. Burrufu leaned down to look at it. It was a painting from Olivia, showing

Burrufu holding her hand next to the words *I love your book.*

Burrufu picked it up, looked at it closely, and felt even worse than ever for what he had said to her.

5. The Tree House

Steve entered Olivia's room to tuck her in like he did every night. He found her already in bed, curled to one side, mad and muttering.

"What's wrong?" he asked. "You've been in a bad mood all day."

"Nothing!" she grumbled.

Steve knew something had happened to her. What father doesn't know when his daughter is mad? But he also knew that Olivia didn't want to talk at that moment.

"All right, sweetie, rest now and you'll see tomorrow that whatever happened today will be better," he said to her before kissing her forehead.

Olivia couldn't sleep. She was still mad at Burrufu. How could he have said such a thing? She hadn't taken anything without permission. *The book was on the floor,* she thought.

She couldn't stop rolling over in bed. When she finally closed her eyes and it looked like she was going to get some sleep, furry feet were trying to silently walk into her room. A furry hand holding a wrapped present was getting closer to the bedside, trying not to make any noise. But it was impossible. Burrufu was more than seven feet tall and very heavy. Even on his tiptoes, he would always make noise.

When Olivia heard the rustling of Burrufu's steps, she opened her eyes wide. She turned, and there was Burrufu, on his tiptoes, looking at her. They remained silent for a moment, just looking at each other.

"I'm sorry," said Burrufu from the bottom of his heart.

Olivia didn't have any evil or grudge in her heart. She never had, and she never would. Her face turned from frowning to her big smile in a second. She stood on her bed and gave him a big hug.

Burrufu was uncomfortable. He did not dare touch her. It's not that he was afraid. It was that personal relationships were new for him. He didn't know what to do or say or how to act with anybody.

"Well, it will be better if I leave," he said, turning to walk out of the room. "I guess you have to sleep."

"Wow, a new book!" She tore the wrapping paper with excitement. "Can you read it to me?" she asked, standing on her bed with the manuscript, looking happily at Burrufu.

Burrufu didn't feel comfortable outside of the attic. Steve was awake and could show up at any moment. Every time he went out, Burrufu made sure no one was around and everyone was sleeping. But this was a special occasion, and he knew that ignoring Olivia's request wouldn't make her stop. He had to accept. "Only one chapter," he said.

Olivia got into bed quick as lightning. She was so excited. Her friend was back, and he was going to read her a book.

Burrufu sat by her side. He put on his little reading glasses and opened the book. "Once upon a time—"

"Hey," Olivia interrupted, "how do you have so many stories? You have so many books in the attic. Are they all yours?"

Burrufu looked at her sadly. "Yes, those are the stories I'd like to live if I had a normal life."

"A normal life?"

"Yes, like you do. Go out to play every day. Talk to people...."

"Don't you ever go outside?" Olivia asked.

"Only at night, when no one can see me. It's safer for everyone."

"Have you ever gone out in the daylight?"

"Do you want me to read or not?" Burrufu insisted.

"Yes, yes, yes—I'm sorry," Olivia answered quickly.

Burrufu continued reading. He was good at it. With his low, deep, reassuring voice, he could make you dream. He had a gift for telling stories. You could see, feel, and even smell everything he was saying. His voice and his words took Olivia to other worlds in her imagination.

A chapter was enough to get Olivia deeply asleep. Burrufu tucked her in, looked at her, and almost smiled.

The next day, Burrufu sat in front of his typewriter writing nonstop, like always. He was absorbed in his thoughts, meditating deeply on each word, when a paper plane flew at his back, straight from the stairs, breaking his concentration.

Who might that be? He thought, as if he didn't know. He opened the plane and found a note from Olivia:

I will pick you up at four o'clock.

Burrufu smiled. And this time it was a full smile. *You cannot beat her at annoyance,* he thought. *At least I have until four o'clock to be calm.*

Time flew, and soon it was four o'clock. As expected, Olivia showed up.

"You're on time," said Burrufu.

"I have a surprise for you," Olivia said as she pulled his hand to make him get up from the desk. It was hard—maybe because Burrufu was heavy or maybe because he wasn't helping her. Olivia went behind him and started pushing him toward the stairs.

"What are you doing? What about your father?" asked Burrufu, very concerned.

"Don't worry. He's working in his office. I promise you he is not going to get out of there."

Olivia kept pulling Burrufu's hand. He wasn't comfortable leaving the attic during the day. They walked down the stairs, through the kitchen and the living room, and arrived at the back door of the house—the door that led to the backyard. Olivia released him and ran to open the door.

"Don't open the door! It's still daylight. Someone could see me," said Burrufu anxiously.

Olivia smiled. "Don't worry. I already thought about that. I'll wait for you in the tree house. Take your time."

Olivia opened the door and ran through a white-walled alley that moved with the wind. Burrufu approached slowly and realized they weren't walls at all. They were sheets. Olivia had created a big white alley from her house to the tree house with ropes and sheets. Now no one could see him. He was safe.

Still nervous, Burrufu took his first step. It was probably the first step he'd taken outside in the daytime in many years. Normally his footsteps made lots of noise, but he made this particular step with such gentleness that it was barely heard. Burrufu's heart was beating stronger with every step he took. He walked slowly, checking that no one could really see him. And with every step he made, the more calm he felt, the more confidence he had, and the bigger he smiled.

At the end of the alley were wooden stairs leading up the tree. They were old planks hammered into the tree itself. The tree house was also covered with sheets. It wasn't very stylish, but it was made with love. Burrufu, still nervous, took a deep breath and started climbing.

"Olivia?" he said in a low voice when he was in the tree house.

"HI!" screamed Olivia with so much enthusiasm that she scared Burrufu, who also screamed and scared Olivia back.

The fright made Burrufu suddenly grow three times his size. *BAM!* He got so big that his arms and legs poked out of the tree house and the roof became Burrufu's hat. Luckily no one from the outside could see thanks to the sheets.

"Olivia? OLIVIA!" yelled Burrufu, surprised and concerned when he couldn't find her.

"Mmmmm...mmm...here!" It was Olivia's voice, but he couldn't see her.

When they had both calmed down, Burrufu shrank to his normal size. He noticed that Olivia was trapped between his back and the sheets.

"That is so cool!" laughed Olivia when Burrufu rescued her and put her on the ground next to poor Tula, scared after what had just happened. Burrufu repaired the roof, fixed the sheets, and sat the best he could. Even at his normal size, he had to bow his head and bend his back. He didn't fit in the small house if he stood up.

"Look, I made cookies." Olivia surprised Burrufu by holding out a plateful of chocolate cookies. It was so full that just a few more would have made it collapse.

His eyes lit up when he saw the cookies. He smiled. They were his favorite kind. He was so happy that he almost couldn't speak. "Th-Th-Th-Thanks," he stuttered, drooling from happiness, and grabbed the plate.

They spent a few hours laughing, having fun, and eating. Their bellies were totally full, even though there were some cookies left on the plate. It was impossible to finish them in one meal.

Later, Burrufu, Olivia, and Tula were resting. Burrufu was half lying down on the floor, and Olivia was resting on his smooth and furry belly, hugging the manuscript he had given her the night before. Like always, she wouldn't stop talking.

Burrufu listened patiently with his eyes closed, keen on taking a nap after the big meal.

"Hey, when you grew before...how did you do it?" Olivia asked. "It's really funny, like the first time I saw you. Can you grow whenever you want to?"

Burrufu opened his eyes, and his smile disappeared. His mood became serious.

"Eh...no," he answered, "it's more complicated than that."

Silence filled the tree house. Burrufu didn't want to talk about it.

Olivia got up and moved in front of his face. "Do you want to know a secret?" she asked as they stared at each other. "The kids from my class say that I'm weird because I don't have a mother, but I don't care because I know that my mother is taking care of me from up above and she loves me the way I am. Sometimes it bothers me that the kids from school pick on me. But I know I'm not weird. I'm just different to them."

Burrufu looked at her with tender eyes. He sat up straight and asked her the same question. "Do you want to know a secret?"

Olivia nodded.

"Do you remember that you were scared the two times I grew?"

"Yep."

"For some reason, when people are scared of me, I grow. And when they stop fearing me, I go back to my normal size. I am weird, too. The bigger I am, the weirder."

"Is all your family the same? Where are your mom and dad?" she asked.

"I don't know," he said. "I've been alone for so long that I don't remember."

"Have you always lived here? Do you have any friends?"

"No," he answered, "but there was one time I went outside in the daylight. I wanted to meet people. It was a long time ago. But I found out that people thought I was weird, and that hurt me."

Olivia kept staring at him.

"It was a bad experience. People were afraid of me, and I grew a lot. I hated myself for being so big. No one likes a monster, and I don't like people."

"I like you," said Olivia with a big smile. "You're not weird, just different."

"OLIVIA?" someone yelled from the ground, interrupting that moment, that connection between them.

Olivia quickly leaned out and saw that it was Mark. "Hi, Mark!" she hollered.

Olivia turned back toward Burrufu and nervously said, "It's Mark! Quick, hide!"

Burrufu was too big to hide in the tree house. There was no place to hide. He was already in the whole tree house. He thought about going out through the windows, but Mark was down on the ground, so that wasn't a good idea. If he tried to get out, Mark would see him.

"I'm coming down!" said Olivia.

"What are these sheets? What are you hiding up there?" asked Mark curiously.

"Nothing, nothing," she nervously answered.

Mark started to climb up the tree house. Burrufu was still there, and he didn't know how to get out.

"Mark, don't come up! I'm going down there!" she yelled, very concerned.

"No, no, you can't fool me...I can smell it from here,"

Mark answered.

Burrufu smelled his armpit. He thought he was clean. He was a monster, but a clean monster.

Just as Mark was about to enter, Olivia covered his head with one of the sheets so that Burrufu could jump out the window without being seen. Before, when Mark was on the ground, that exit would have given Burrufu away, but now that Mark was in the house with his face covered, Burrufu could safely escape the tree house.

"Olivia, what are you doing?" asked Mark in surprise, removing the sheet from his face.

"I knew it!" he exclaimed. "Cookies! My sense of smell has never let me down." Mark rushed in and ate a few of the cookies that were left on the plate.

"Mmm, so good. Listen, have you thought of selling these?" Mark asked with his mouth full.

Olivia sighed. "No, I'm not like you," she joked.

"Let me suggest something," he continued while he was chewing. "If your father doesn't finish the book, we could build the Mark and Olivia's Cookie Company."

"But I make them by myself! Why would they have your name?"

"Well, because it's my idea!" Mark laughed as they climbed down the tree to go inside the house.

In all the rush and nervousness, no one noticed that the manuscript Olivia had been holding was still in the tree house.

Hours later, Mark was saying good-bye to Steve. "Remember, I need your book as soon as possible. I need to be rich now!"

"Yes, don't be such a pest!" laughed Steve, closing the door. Through the closed door, Mark heard Steve yelling, "Olivia! What are all those sheets in the backyard?"

When Mark was about to leave in his van, he remembered that there were a few more cookies left in the tree house. He thought about taking them for the ride. He climbed up the planks, avoiding getting stuck in the sheets. The plate was there, and there were a few left. *Good enough,* he thought. He took them, and as he was leaving, he discovered the manuscript they had forgotten. He grabbed it, leafed through it, and took it with him, thinking it was Steve's or maybe Olivia's. Who else's could it be?

A whole day passed. Burrufu locked himself in the attic. He didn't want to go out. Mark had almost discovered him. He was nervous. The feeling of going out was amazing, and he was truly thankful for Olivia's gesture, but he almost got caught, and that made him feel uncomfortable. Burrufu looked at the tree house from his window. It was still covered with the sheets. It made him smile.

The following night, almost at midnight, Olivia was already asleep when Burrufu entered her room quietly. He was trying not to make noise because Olivia's dad was still awake and working in his office.

_{"Are you awake?"} he whispered. Olivia opened her eyes wide. A big smile appeared on her face, and she nodded.

"Would you like to see the sea?" he asked Olivia.

Olivia, very surprised, said, "The sea? But it's far away. It would take a long time to get there."

Burrufu smiled. He took out two orange wool caps, the kind that cover your ears and tie under your chin. There was one for him and one for her. Olivia's was big, but she didn't care. It looked like Burrufu didn't only write. He made caps, too. With so much time and solitude, he had to find hobbies.

"What if someone sees us?" asked Olivia, worried. "I wouldn't like something like yesterday to happen again."

Burrufu calmed her down. "At this hour, the whole town is sleeping, and no one lives where we are going." He picked up Olivia and put her on his back.

"What about Tula?" she asked.

"Not tonight. Another time."

"But where are we going?"

"Just hold on to me, sweetie."

Burrufu opened the window and sat on the ledge. Olivia held on to the fur on his back.

"Are you ready?" he asked.

Olivia looked down. She saw the height and held even tighter, just in case. She closed her eyes and nodded because she could barely talk.

Burrufu grabbed the edge of the window, leaned back to get up speed, and jumped—and jumped and jumped! He jumped so high that they moved far from the house very quickly. In a few strides, Burrufu could cover hundreds of feet. They were traveling very fast, and wind softly touched Olivia's face. She still had her eyes closed.

After a while, while Burrufu was still jumping, Olivia opened her eyes and saw a completely new landscape. It was spectacular. Everything was blurry because of the speed, but it was still stunning. A great feeling of excitement and happiness filled her body. She couldn't stop smiling.

Burrufu kept jumping and jumping until they arrived at the top of a hill, where, by the soft light of the full moon, Olivia could see tall jagged mountains and dark ocean waves. The view amazed her. She had never been to this place before, and at that moment she fell in love with those trees, that sea, those hills, the smell of the grass, the sound of the wind moving the leaves...everything.

"Do you want to hear a new story?" asked Burrufu, pulling one of his manuscripts from his fur.

Olivia looked at him, smiled, and nodded. She was still feeling so amazed that she couldn't say a word. She felt like she was dreaming, and she didn't want to wake up.

After a few hours, Olivia was half asleep in Burrufu's warm and furry lap, and he was looking out at the sea in silence. *It's time to leave,* he thought. *Olivia should be sleeping in her bed.*

Burrufu tried not to wake her, but when he got up, Olivia with her eyes still closed asked, "Will you be my friend forever?"

Burrufu looked at her the way a grandfather looks at his granddaughter. His eyes were full of tenderness and love. Olivia had been the only person to soften Burrufu's hard heart and the only one to get him out of the house in a long time.

For Olivia, it was the easiest thing to do, because she loved him just for what he was—no more, no less. She never demanded anything. She never asked him to change. She just accepted him for being Burrufu.

"Of course I will," answered Burrufu with kindness.

"Will you pick me up at school?" murmured Olivia, almost asleep.

Burrufu kept quiet for a second. He looked at her, and while he played with her hair he answered, "I will, for sure."

Olivia smiled and fell asleep.

Burrufu arrived at the house with Olivia completely asleep in his arms. He went in through the same window he had used to go out and put Olivia in her bed. Her father, who was still working, heard the noises Burrufu was trying to avoid making.

"Olivia?" he asked, surprised.

When Burrufu heard Steve approaching, he got nervous and thought about getting out of the room very fast. But he was so unlucky that the manuscript he was holding fell to the floor. Burrufu noticed it but didn't have time to pick it up because Steve was about to walk in. The only thing he could do was duck into the closet. Burrufu could barely fit. He was trying not to move because he didn't want to make any noise. Through the gaps of the door, Burrufu could see what was happening in the room.

Steve saw his daughter sleeping. He tucked her in and kissed her good night.

As he was leaving, he tripped over Burrufu's manuscript. He crouched down and picked it up. Burrufu, who was watching, held his breath. Luckily, Steve didn't pay much attention to what it was. He just glanced through the pages and put it on the bedside table.

Burrufu exhaled with relief.

When Steve was gone, Burrufu got out of the closet very quietly and picked up his manuscript. *It's better not to go through the door,* he thought. So he climbed out the window and across the roof to the little window of the attic.

6. Pleased To Meet You

Very early the following day, while Olivia was still sleeping, someone banged on the front door. It was Mark.

"Steve! Steve! Open the door!" he hollered urgently.

The knocks mixed in with Tula's barks. She acted very nervous every time someone was on the other side of the door.

Steve was in the kitchen. He was dressed better than usual, holding his coffee in one hand and his newspaper under his arm. He got up to see who was making so much noise. "Tula, stop barking."

When he opened the door, Steve was surprised to find Mark. His old friend seemed excited and nervous, almost trembling with emotion. Although usually well dressed, at that moment Mark's hair was sticking up in certain spots, his shirt was untucked, and his jacked was rumpled. It was weird to see Steve all dressed up and Mark all scruffy . It had always been the opposite.

"What's wrong, Mark?" Steve asked nervously. "The interview is in one hour."

"Forget the interview!" said Mark in a choked voice. "Your new book...I...I..."

"You what?"

"I LOVE IT! It's...it's...AMAZING!" Mark hugged Steve with some force. "Thanks, thanks, thanks..."

"What are you talking about?" asked Steve, trying to get out of the hug. "Every day you get weirder."

"It's...it's...your book. What, what...what a story, what characters...what EVERYTHING!"

Olivia came down the stairs in her pajamas, rubbing the sleep from her eyes. "What's wrong with Mark?"

"Sadly, nothing," Steve said ironically. "He's like always."

Steve and Olivia went into the kitchen to have breakfast as if Mark wasn't even there. They were more than used to his moments of madness. He was invisible to them. Steve poured himself more coffee and brought milk and cereal to Olivia. "You'll have to get dressed right after breakfast, honey. The people from the TV show are coming to record us, and I want you to look nice."

"The TV interview!" Olivia had almost forgotten about it.

Mark was freaking out. No one was listening to him. Steve and Olivia acted like he wasn't even there. He looked at them in astonishment. No one cared.

"Steve, Steve, listen," Mark interrupted. "You have to let me publish this now. We'll be rich. I will make you rich. I'll be rich!"

"Mark! I don't know what you're talking about."

"Okay, okay, I'll lower my percentages. You'll get more. But don't leave me out of this, please!" Mark begged, taking hold of Steve's leg.

"I repeat, I. Don't. Know. What. You. Are. Talking. About," said Steve very seriously.

Mark laughed. "What am I...?" Mark looked at Steve like he was the weird one. He looked at Olivia, back to Steve, then to Tula, trying to exchange looks with at least one pair of understanding eyes. "What am I talking about? I'm talking about this."

Mark pulled from his briefcase the manuscript he'd found in the tree house.

Steve took it and started to flip through it with curiosity.

Olivia realized that it was Burrufu's manuscript! She didn't know what to do. If she said or did anything, she would give herself away and everything would come to light. So she gulped her whole glass of milk, jumped off the chair, pretending nothing was going on, and went to her room. She didn't run, because it would have raised suspicion, but she walked quickly. She had to get out of the kitchen.

"That's weird," said Steve pensively. "I think I've seen something like this not too long ago.... Olivia!" He called her just as she reached her room.

"Yes?" She turned nervously and walked slowly back to the kitchen.

"Do you know something about this?" her father asked, showing her Burrufu's manuscript.

"No," she answered, "why would I?"

"Because I saw another one like this in your room yesterday. It was on the floor, and I put it on your bedside table."

"Is there another book?" Mark mumbled to himself, very excited.

"I don't know what you're talking about, Dad."
Olivia was concerned.

Steve headed to Olivia's room to solve the mystery once and for all. Of course, Mark went after him. If there was another manuscript, Mark wanted to get his hands on it.

Olivia was getting nervous because they were going to find another of Burrufu's books. When Steve entered the room, he looked everywhere—on the bedside table, behind, below, along the sides, under the bed—but he couldn't find anything.

"Where is it, Olivia?" asked Mark, very serious.

"I don't know what you're talking about," she repeated nervously.

"Olivia, come here." Steve sat on the bed and took her by the hand to calm her down and get her to answer truthfully. "Whose book is this?"

"It's...it's...it's..." She didn't know how to answer.

"Honey, you've always told me everything", he said looking into her eyes. "You know you can trust me, right?"

"Yes," answered Olivia in a very, very low voice.

"Did you steal it?"

"No!" she quickly interrupted. "No, no! It's...it's a gift."

"A manuscript? No one gives a manuscript. This is too important to give as a gift," Steve told her. "Olivia, tell me the truth."

"It is the truth, Dad," she insisted. "It's a gift from my best friend."

Steve was running out of patience. "And who is this new best friend?"

"I can't tell you. I promised that I wouldn't."

Steve sighed. He got up from the bed and prepared to leave the room. "All right, you're grounded."

"But Dad!" Olivia exclaimed.

"When you learn to be responsible and tell the truth, we'll talk." He looked at Olivia for a second, and when she didn't respond, he started closing the door.

"Burrufu," she said in a tiny voice just before he closed the door completely.

"What's that?" he asked.

"His name is Burrufu," she said, feeling guilty, helpless, and angry all at once.

"Olivia, this is a very serious matter. A manuscript is something very important to a writer. You should know that. I don't like you kidding about this, much less lying to me."

"You have to promise me that if I tell you, you won't get mad," demanded Olivia with an angry frown.

Steve and Mark looked at each other in surprise. Steve didn't know what else he had to say to Olivia to make her tell the truth.

"And promise me you won't do anything weird," she added.

Steve bent over to Olivia's height. "Why should I, sweetie?"

"Promise me! And also you, Mark. You won't do anything strange, okay?"

"Yes, yes, I promise," answered Mark.

Olivia stared at her dad with her sad face, looking for understanding and love. Steve nodded.

Olivia walked into the hallway. Steve and Mark followed her. When they reached the corridor with the hidden door, Olivia looked once again to her father, took a deep breath, and triggered the lamp.

The door opened, and Olivia went up the stairs to the attic.

When her father saw the secret door, he froze. He hadn't known that was in the house. He didn't know where those stairs lead to, and he also didn't know where Olivia had gone.

Steve and Mark heard Olivia's and Burrufu's voices. They looked at each other, disconcerted. For them, that low, deep voice that was talking to Olivia was still unknown.

"I don't want to go outside!" said Burrufu from the attic.

"It's okay, nothing will happen," Olivia responded. "It's my father and his best friend. They'll understand. Please, do it for me."

The argument continued for a few minutes.

"Olivia?" asked Steve in a shaky voice as he approached the stairs.

Olivia went down quickly to avoid anyone going up. "Dad, remember that you promised you weren't going to get scared."

"What are you talking about? Scared of what? I promised I wouldn't get mad," he answered, very nervous.

"Okay, now promise me you won't get scared," Olivia begged.

"Okay, okay."

"It's okay! You can come down!" Olivia yelled from the hallway to the attic.

The house was calm. No one could hear anything. Not even Tula made noise. It was like that for a minute. They all looked at one another.

Then, something started coming slowly down the stairs.

BAM!

BAM!

Steve and Mark were getting more nervous. They didn't know what was approaching.

BAM!

BAM!

The steps were big and heavy. Furry feet with huge nails emerged from the dark. With each step, more of Burrufu's body appeared....

BAM!

BAM!

Until he was completely in the light.

Steve was petrified. Mark's briefcase fell from his hands.

No one said anything until Burrufu broke the silence. "Hi," he greeted them politely.

Neither Steve nor Mark dared to say a word.

"Pleased to meet you, sirs," Burrufu continued.

Steve was nervous, so much that he started to tremble in fear.

Burrufu knew that something like this would happen. That's why he hadn't wanted to come out of hiding. *This was a bad idea,* he thought. Burrufu started to be afraid of the fear he was creating. He didn't want to get big.

"Please, don't be afraid," he said to the adults as he approached them. As bad luck would have it, they got more scared.

Burrufu, nervous, started to get bigger and bigger, which made them even more frightened.

"Dad, calm down. It's okay. He's my best friend," Olivia said, trying to smooth things over.

"No, no, nooo, noooo! It's a monster!" exclaimed Steve. Without hesitation, he took Olivia into his arms and started running, full of fear, down the stairs and toward the street.

Olivia screamed, "Dad, no! Put me down! He's my best friend! He won't hurt you!"

Mark, who was still upstairs with Burrufu, also started to run. "A MONSTER!" he screamed.

Olivia began to cry. "BURRUFU!" she yelled. "I'M SORRY!"

Burrufu, also nervous, ran hastily into the attic, mad at himself, at Olivia, at the situation. "I knew something like this was going to happen," he said to himself. "I'll never go out again!"

He looked at the mirror, and when he saw his reflection, so big, so giant, he was disgusted. He shattered the mirror with a hard punch. He didn't want to see himself ever again. Burrufu roared, filled with rage and helplessness.

Steve had managed to open the door and escape into the street with Olivia still in his arms. But just at that moment, he stumbled into the reporter, the camera operators, and a few technicians from the network who were going to interview him.

"Mr. Norby?" asked the reporter, "are you feeling all right?"

Steve didn't answer. He was still stunned by and absorbed in what he had seen.

The reporter got closer to Steve's face. "Mr. Norby?"

Steve could only stutter. "Mons-Mons-Mons-"

Mark came running out of the house screaming, "A MONSTER!"

Olivia was trying to get rid of her father and get back inside the house. She wanted to ask for Burrufu's forgiveness and be by his side. He was her best friend. She had to. But her father was standing in her way.

Olivia wouldn't stop screaming Burrufu's name.

Burrufu looked at her through the window and cursed the day he had met her.

Her father, almost hysterical by now, asked the reporter to call the police, the fire department, and the army. "Someone, for God's sake!"

The reporter, not knowing what to do, simply agreed. The technicians and the camera operators didn't know what to do either, so they started to do their job and record everything that was happening.

Complete chaos broke out in a few seconds. People on the street gathered to look at the two men screaming. Some cars stopped, making others honk. Steve grabbed the reporter. Tula was barking. Mark, scared, tried to hide in his van. It was mayhem.

The moment his attention strayed, Olivia finally got away from her father and started running toward the house. She was trying to avoid everyone because she didn't want to get caught. She started crossing the street to shake everyone off, but she tripped over the wires coming out of the reporter's van and fell in the middle of the road. At that moment, a truck, trying to avoid the traffic jam, was barreling toward her.

The driver didn't see her, and he didn't have time to react. Everyone helplessly watched the terrible scene unfold. The truck was about to run her over.

BAM!

Smoke started pouring from the engine. Something had come between the truck and Olivia. Something had prevented the tragedy.

Burrufu.

He had jumped without any hesitation to save Olivia, breaking the window and even part of the wall. Burrufu knew he could take the impact of the truck. That's why he had done it. He sacrificed his hideout for Olivia's protection.

All the noise from the chaos died away. Silence fell. Everyone was stunned when they saw Burrufu. No one knew what to do. The camera operators who were recording everything kept rolling even though their legs trembled in fear of Burrufu.

The reporter started screaming. The kids on the street began to cry and run to their houses.

The technicians hopped in the van as fast as they could. Steve ran toward Olivia to get her away from Burrufu.

Burrufu turned and looked at the fear he was causing. He started to grow and grow without stopping.

Nervous, Burrufu started to run to get out of there. But the fear was so great that he grew to more than thirty feet tall. Every step he took, the more people he found and the more people he scared, making him grow more and more.

When he was a hundred feet tall, he knew there was nowhere to hide. Everywhere he went, whatever he did, he could still be seen by hundreds of people. He was a giant.

But for some reason, Burrufu stopped growing. It seemed that a hundred feet, almost as tall as a ten-story building, was his maximum height.

Chaos took over the city. No one was calm. Everyone who saw Burrufu ran away in terror, scared to death.

Poor Burrufu. Scared, mad, and furious, he didn't know what to do or where to go. He decided to keep still in the center of the city. Anywhere he went, people were going to see him. Why hide? His heart was filled with pain and sadness. He didn't want to cause fear.

He didn't have evil inside him. Maybe that sadness made him want to surrender and not escape.

Emergency services arrived and behaved like they had to save the city from Burrufu. It was odd because he would never hurt anyone, but no one knew that.

And that was because no one, apart from Olivia, knew him. Sadly, when met with the unknown, most people's first reaction is fear.

They don't notice that maybe they are standing in front of their new best friend.

Police sealed off the area where Burrufu was seated. Firefighters were prepared for any situation. And a few minutes later, the military arrived with their guns, tanks, and everything else. Without a word and without wasting a second, they started to shoot him. They wanted to destroy that weird thing, whatever it was.

Burrufu didn't move. Luckily, nothing could harm him. His skin was so fatty and soft that even bullets could not go through it. The military kept shooting without getting anywhere. Burrufu didn't offer resistance.

Olivia arrived in the van with Steve and Mark. She jumped out while the van was practically still moving and ran to defend Burrufu, to protect her friend.

"No! Please, stop!" she screamed without success. Olivia was trying to stop the soldiers, but no one listened to her. Who would listen to a little girl? Steve picked her up to protect her.

Among all those soldiers, anything could happen to her.

One soldier approached them and rudely kicked them out.

"Burrufu!" screamed Olivia in despair.

Burrufu looked at her with sad eyes. He already knew what was going to happen to him, as if it had all happened before.

More military trucks came from everywhere, as well as more police, more firefighters. All of them were there. Soldiers climbed down from their trucks with big boxes. They organized very quickly and started to give every soldier, police officer, and firefighter a smoke bomb, nets, ropes, and anything else they thought they could use.

People were still screaming when they saw Burrufu, and Olivia cried, powerless at what was happening. "Defend yourself! Do something!" she screamed. "Get out of here, please! Run!"

Burrufu did nothing. Knowing that he was the reason for those people's screams broke his heart.

However, there was one thing he didn't know. It wasn't him. It was prejudice. If people would get to know him like Olivia did, they would soon realize that there was no reason to be afraid.

"Now!" ordered one of the army generals.

In that moment, dozens of smoke bombs flew at Burrufu. A big white cloud formed around his face, and Burrufu started to cough. That cloud, full of sleep-inducer, knocked him unconscious.

7. Don't Be Afraid

By the time night arrived, the chaos was over. The city was trying to go back to normal. Emergency services and the military were planning how to handle the situation. Olivia and her father were taken by two soldiers to a tent used as an interrogation room where a general and a man with a white coat waited for them.

The general, a strong and serious old man with a big white mustache and lots of medals on his chest, started to interrogate Olivia without compassion. He was rough and rude. His only motivation was to get all the answers about the supposed *menace* that Burrufu was.

However, the other man, the one in the white coat, worked for some kind of secret scientific organization, supposedly for the government, and wanted to *understand* the monster, to study him.

"Where did you meet the monster?" started the general.

"He's not a monster!" Olivia answered angrily. "He's my friend. His name is Burrufu."

The general looked at the soldiers with skepticism.

"How long have you known this...Burrufu?" said the man in the white coat, more kindly.

"Can I see him?" asked Olivia.

"No! Right now he is a menace, and we don't know what he can do," answered the general severely.

"Can I see him?" Olivia asked again, this time looking at the man in the white coat.

He had better manners and answered politely. "You'll see him if you answer some questions first."

"But I want to see him. He's my friend," begged Olivia.

"I'm sorry, but right now it's not allowed any kind of contact."

"But he's my friend. Please..."

"Look," continued the kind man in the white coat, "tell me everything, and I'll see what I can do, okay?"

Olivia nodded, full of hope of seeing Burrufu again.

They spoke for a long time in that tent. Olivia told them the whole story of how she met Burrufu and all the details she could recall—his books, the trip to the sea, the tree house....

Listening to his daughter, Steve realized how wrong he had been, how he had prejudged Burrufu. He should have gotten to know him first.

The general, outraged, thought they were wasting their time listening to Olivia because he still didn't know how to eliminate what he believed was a menace. The general wouldn't let them see Burrufu, but luckily, the man in the white coat seemed to have more power than the general. He convinced the general to leave Olivia alone with Burrufu for a few minutes. After all, the monster couldn't possibly escape.

The general left the tent with Olivia and Steve and ordered a corporal to go with them to the sealed-off zone. They walked by dozens of military tents set up all over the sector where Burrufu had fallen.

They went through one last checkpoint where only one private stood guard. Burrufu was totally tied down and still drugged. That broke Olivia's heart. To see her best friend like that wasn't easy.

The corporal left them to the young soldier's watch. "Eh, Private! Here, I've brought these two. They have the general's permission to see the monster."

"Y-Y-Yes...siiiiir!" answered the private, trembling. He couldn't stop shaking. His legs, his gun, his helmet...everything was shaking. Maybe that was the reason why Burrufu couldn't shrink.

Olivia's father stopped next to the private and let Olivia get close to Burrufu. When she reached his side, she realized Burrufu's head was as big as a truck.

"Burrufu?" said Olivia in a sweet voice.

Burrufu opened his eyes, but when he saw her, he turned his head away to avoid looking into her eyes.

"I'm so sorry about everything," Olivia continued. "It was all my fault."

Burrufu kept silent.

Olivia reached out to touch him when Burrufu spoke in a wounded voice. "It'd be better if you leave."

Olivia started crying. She felt terrible for what had happened to Burrufu. She didn't know what to do. She turned to her father, looking for an answer, for any advice.

Steve felt sorry for his daughter, for everything that had happened. If he hadn't run away, if he hadn't called Burrufu a monster, if he'd listened to Olivia, this wouldn't have happened.

Steve walked over to the private, who was still shaking. "Hi."

"H-H-Hi, s-s-ssir!" answered the private.

"Hey, look, why don't you go and drink some decaf tea? That way you could relax a little bit," Steve hinted, hoping the private would leave the tent.

"I ca...I can't, sir. I can't a-a-abandon my place. I'm f-f-following orders, sir."

Steve tried to convince him by any means possible.

"Look, I know you're afraid, and in this situation, the best thing you can do is go outside and calm yourself. If you're worried about my daughter, I can take care of her."

"O-o-okay, I guess some tea won't do any harm," said the private, very relieved. "If something happens, please call me and don't tell anyone else." He sighed, placed his gun in his belt, and thanked Steve.

Once he checked that they were alone, Steve got close to Burrufu. "Thanks," he said kindly, "for saving my daughter."

Burrufu still had his head turned away, but when he heard Steve's voice, he turned and looked into his eyes. He found sincerity.

"You told me you would always be by my side," said Olivia, weeping.

Burrufu turned to her. "I can't be with you! I'm a monster!" he exclaimed.

"No...you're not." Olivia got closer. "You're my best friend. And friends are forever." At that moment, Olivia hugged Burrufu's nose because it was the only thing she could grab. "You're my friend," she said, sobbing.

"Olivia, look at me," said Burrufu quietly. "People are scared just to see me. I'm a giant monster."

She moved from his nose to look into his eyes.

"Don't worry," continued Burrufu, "it's not your fault. It's just the way it is. I was born like this."

Olivia stared at him. "No, things are not like that. They don't have to be," she said wiping her tears and runny nose with the sleeve of her shirt.

"I've always been big and ugly," said Burrufu with weepy eyes. "People have always been scared of me."

Olivia looked closely at him. "Not me. I've never been afraid of you."

Burrufu laughed. "You're not afraid of *anything*! You're a very brave girl."

Olivia, still with tears in her eyes, wouldn't stop looking at Burrufu. "You are my Burrufu, and I love you the way you are."

Even Steve couldn't stop his tears. The situation was painfully unfair.

Suddenly, in that moment, something happened.

Burrufu was getting smaller! He became smaller and smaller until all the chains and ropes that had him captured grew loose. They were too big for him. They were for a hundred-foot monster, and now he was only seven feet.

They all looked at one another in surprise. "What just happened?" Olivia asked.

"I guess," said Steve, "no one here is afraid of you." Steve approached Burrufu and gave him his hand as a gesture of friendship.

Everyone smiled. Olivia jumped into Burrufu's arms, and he hugged her tight.

"This was all my fault, so I'll help you out of here," said Steve.

8. The Escape

"Help! Somebody help me!" Steve cried out nervously.

Olivia was lying on the floor. The young soldier relaxing with his tea threw everything away when he heard the noise and ran back to his post.

"What happened?" asked the soldier, but before anyone could answer, he looked around in surprise. "W-W-W-Where is the monster?"

Burrufu was gone. There were only chains on the floor.

"Who cares about that!" Steve screamed. "My daughter is seriously wounded! We need an ambulance!"

The soldier didn't react, and he nervously looked for Burrufu in the sky.

Steve grabbed him by the shirt. "That's not important right now, soldier! My daughter could die any moment! Go find an ambulance!"

The soldier went running, looking for an ambulance. Steve, Olivia, and Burrufu, who was hiding inside a garbage container, smiled. Everything was going to be okay.

wEEEOOOOoEEEwEEEOOOOoEEE!

The soldier had just activated the alarm!

What were all smiles a second ago became worried faces.

Hundreds of soldiers came from everywhere with emergency lights and search spotlights. Everybody was staring at the sky, looking for a giant monster. Luckily, no one was paying attention to the ground. Their gazes were aiming up.

"What should we do now, Daddy?" whispered Olivia, still pretending to be unconscious.

"I don't know, I don't know," Steve said, worried.

Burrufu was looking through a small hole in the garbage container at the soldiers now filling the place where, just a few moments ago, he had been completely chained.

The young soldier came with a military ambulance to *save* Olivia.

According to Steve, the plan was to hide Burrufu in the ambulance in the middle of the chaos and escape. Obviously he wouldn't fit in a car. That's why they needed something big.

The general saw the ambulance and called over the soldier. He didn't understand if they were looking for a monster, why they needed an ambulance. "Private, what's all this?"

"It's the girl," he replied. "She's badly wounded."

"The girl!" shouted the general. "I knew it! Where is she?"

The soldier pointed to the place where Olivia was pretending to be passed out. But there was no one there. Steve and Olivia had hidden inside the garbage container with Burrufu, just before the general could see them.

The general was looking all over for them. "Bring me that girl and her father, or you'll be scrubbing toilets until my retirement!"

"Yes, sir." The soldier swallowed hard and ran.

"What a great plan, Dad," Olivia said ironically.

"Don't worry. The moment we can, we'll get inside the ambulance and..." Before he could finish, they saw the soldier who had brought the ambulance drive it away.

"What now?" asked Burrufu.

"Now?" Steve said. "Now...RUN!"

They ran with their heads down through one of the back alleys, where there were no soldiers.

At the end of the alley, it looked like they could escape. Soldiers continued filling the streets, but all of them were looking at the sky, searching for a colossal monster.

When they reached the end of the alley, something came between them and escape. They heard the sound of a van braking next to them, and just in case, they all raised their arms in surrender. Perhaps it was soldiers in one of the trucks, aiming at them.

"Finally, I find you!" It was Mark with his van. Steve had never been so happy to see him in all of his life.

"Mark!" he shouted as he happily hugged his old friend. But just that second, he realized if Mark saw Burrufu, he'd be scared. And if Mark was scared,

Burrufu would get bigger, and the soldiers would find out where he was.

"No, no, no, go away! Burrufu is here," said Steve, nervously.

"Perfect. He's the one I want to talk to," answered Mark.

Nobody understood what was going on. Olivia and her father looked at each other in surprise. Mark moved them out of his way and headed toward Burrufu. Although he was no longer afraid of him, Mark approached him very carefully. Burrufu still commanded respect.

Burrufu, who was more concerned and nervous than Mark, didn't want to look at his face. He didn't want Mark to get scared.

"Your book..." Mark started to say in a nervous and excited voice. "It's amazing. Please, let me be your editor."

Burrufu turned toward him. He couldn't understand why Mark wasn't afraid anymore.

Steve approached Mark with skepticism. "Aren't you afraid of him anymore?"

"Afraid? Me? Of him?" Mark had a huge smile on his face. "How could I be afraid of the man who's going to make me rich?" He hugged Burrufu in excitement.

Burrufu didn't know what to do. It was a weird situation. Well, maybe not so weird for Mark.

"I don't think now is the time," said Steve, trying to move Burrufu. "We have to get away from here."

All of them piled into Mark's van.

"Perfect, you drive," Mark said to Steve, throwing him the keys. "Burrufu—it's Burrufu, right? So...Burrufu, we should talk business."

Steve didn't want to argue, so he grabbed the keys and sat in the driver's seat. Olivia, Burrufu, and Mark hid in the rear. Steve started to drive slowly so they wouldn't draw any attention.

Just as they were about to exit the sealed-off zone, a soldier signaled them to stop.

"Hide!" warned Steve as they approached the soldier.

"You're not allowed to be here, sir," said the soldier.

"I know, I know. Sorry, I got lost."

Unfortunately, while Steve was talking to the soldier, a military car followed by a truck filled with soldiers drove by. Inside that car was the angry general who had previously questioned Olivia, and he was looking for them. He turned, by chance, and recognized Steve right away.

"There they are!" yelled the general. "Soldier, arrest them!"

The soldier talking to Steve took out his gun and told Steve to get out of the van. Without hesitation, Steve stepped on the gas and fled.

"Follow them!" screamed the general.

And the chase began. Trucks, motorcycles, cars, anything that could go fast pursued the van. All the soldiers were after them. Even the one who had pulled the gun hopped into a car.

Steve drove as fast as he could, but he was not an expert in escaping at top speed. He drove on the sidewalk. He crashed through trash cans and even mailboxes. Luckily for everyone, most of the people were hiding in their houses. Finally, they arrived at the outskirts of the city and drove toward the woods. Maybe they could hide among the trees. But the military was right behind them, filling the road with their green-and-brown vehicles.

Steve tried to go faster, but even with his foot all the way down on the pedal, the van just couldn't go any faster. They were carrying too much weight.

The military cars were getting closer and closer. In fact, they were so close that they started hitting the van to make them lose control or stop. Mark started to scream hysterically.

"Dad, what are we going to do?" asked Olivia, who was feeling really nervous.

"I don't know, honey," he replied with concern.

At one point, the van was filled with bumps and screams. It seemed like they were going to go off the road.

Burrufu took control of the situation. "Hang on tight!"

"What are you going to do?" asked Olivia.

"I'm going to scare them."

"But you'll get bigger," Olivia said, worried.

Burrufu looked at her, smiling and full of confidence. "I know."

He opened wide the rear doors and roared like he never had before. Cars stopped immediately, sharply braking, their drivers panicking. Their fear was so great that they would rather stop than continue chasing Burrufu.

Burrufu started to become bigger and bigger. More cars approached from behind those who had stopped. In one of those cars was the general, giving orders. "Shoot! Shoot! Do anything to stop them!"

The soldiers resumed their chasing. They had to because they were following orders, but their fear grew inside them. Their hands were shaking while driving.

Burrufu, who was already double his usual size, didn't fit in Mark's van any longer, so he stepped out and started running by its side.

Most of the soldiers were really scared, so Burrufu kept growing and growing, and his strides were big enough to follow the van's speed. By now he was so big he could grab the van like a football.

With the van tucked safely under his arm, Burrufu started running and jumping as high and as far as he could, leaving all the cars and trucks behind. They were so far behind that within a few seconds, all of them had disappeared.

Olivia, Steve, and Mark were cheering inside the van because they'd escaped safe and sound. They couldn't stop hanging on to anything, though, because Burrufu's jumps made the van dip up and down like a roller coaster.

9. Farewell

Dawn was coming. Everything was quiet, and luckily they had lost everyone who had been chasing them. Burrufu, who was finally getting smaller, parked the van on the top of the same hill he had taken Olivia to see the sea the night before.

Olivia brought Burrufu his scarf. It had fallen off when he grew big, and she had picked it up.

The four of them were seated, staring at the sunrise, resting from the rush of adrenaline. Olivia was so thrilled, hugged by her friend. Everyone was happy knowing they had escaped.

"We have to think of something to fix this for good," said Steve.

Burrufu remained silent.

"I'll go to the media tomorrow, and I'll tell them..." Steve thought it over. "Rats! I don't know what I am going to say."

Mark got up and approached Burrufu. "Hey, if you'd let me be your editor, people would know you."

"Now is not the time, Mark," Steve interrupted.

"No, no, I mean it. It'd be good for him. If people could read what he writes, they wouldn't be afraid of him since they'd identify themselves in his words. Really, if they read what I read...."

Everyone looked at Mark expectantly.

Mark made an effort to find the right words. "He would no longer be a stranger to them. They would realize he is like us. He is *one* of us."

Olivia felt very happy about this idea. She had saved her best friend, and Mark had come up with the perfect plan to introduce Burrufu to society. That idea seemed perfect!

"When we get home, we'll fix this mess. You'll see. People will know you, and no one will be afraid of you anymore," said Olivia, delighted.

Burrufu looked down. "I can't go."

Olivia looked at him. She didn't understand what he was talking about.

"Thanks, Mark, but I don't think it will work. People won't see past what I look like."

"But—" said Olivia.

"Honey, you have to understand that if I return, this will happen again. For them, I am a monster."

"We'll convince them that you're harmless," Steve interrupted.

"Thank you all, really, thanks. But if I come back with you, your lives would be in danger." Burrufu turned to Olivia and continued, "And that's the last thing I want."

Olivia's eyes filled with tears, and she began to cry uncontrollably. She hugged him so tightly, almost too much for her small hands.

"No, no...please...don't do that to me," Olivia pleaded as she wept.

"Don't worry, my dear. This isn't the first time this has happened to me. I'll come visit once in a while...when everything has calmed down."

Burrufu lifted Olivia to the same level as his head. "Take care. And read everything I left for you in the attic. I want to know if you like it."

Olivia looked at him through her tears. She didn't want to say good-bye.

Burrufu hugged her. "Thanks for everything."

Steve came over and picked up Olivia in his arms. She would never have let go of Burrufu on her own.

Burrufu turned to Mark. "If you want to, you can publish what's in the attic. But do me a favor. Make Olivia the author."

After that he turned to Steve. "Your novel is very good, Steve. You're a very talented writer. Polish up the fifth chapter so it's not so clichéd, and everything will be better."

Finally, he turned to Olivia again. "You are also my best friend." He fondly touched Olivia's little nose with his.

Burrufu turned away. He said good-bye one last time and jumped, jumped, and jumped until he disappeared behind the hills, just as the sun finished rising.

Olivia kept crying and looked at the hill where Burrufu had disappeared.

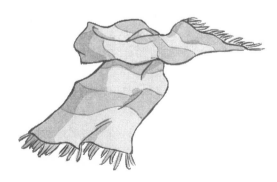

10. More Cookies

Years went by—lots of years. Olivia grew up and became a woman. She still wore dresses but now she wore her hair pulled back with a headband.

She was sitting on a bench on the same hill where, many years ago, she had said good-bye to Burrufu. Everything had changed. Now there were buildings where before there had been only trees. The hills were dotted with houses and stores, and stone roads covered the grass.

The silence of that place had disappeared. It had been replaced with the typical noises of a small city: people selling fruits in farmers' markets, cars running, passengers hopping on a streetcar, kids playing and laughing.

Right in front of Olivia was a small and beautiful park where kids ran, old men chatted, and lovers walked and cuddled.

Olivia was reading a book on the bench. She was smiling, completely immersed in the pages, when a little girl who had been playing in the park approached and interrupted her reading.

"Mommy, Mommy," said the little girl.

Olivia marked the page she was reading with the picture she had taken of Burrufu many years ago in their first encounter, when she was wearing her kitchen armor.

She looked up and smiled at her daughter. "Tell me, honey."

"Shall we go home?" asked the little girl.

"Why do you want to go home so soon?"

"I want to bake some cookies."

Olivia smiled. "Okay, let's go." She got up and took her little girl by the hand.

They were walking home on the stone sidewalk when the little girl asked, "do you think he likes the ones that I bake?"

"Has he ever not eaten a cookie?" Olivia asked.

"I know," answered the little girl, smiling. "He always eats them all."

The End

My Monster Burrufu by Alberto Corral
Published by Petite Grande Idée
petitegrandeidee.com
Los Angeles, California

E-mail us at:
info@petitegrandeidee.com

Don't forget to visit:
mymonsterburrufu.com

Like us at:
facebook.com/mymonsterburrufu

PETITE GRANDE IDÉE

CPSIA information can be obtained at www.ICGtesting.com
Printed in the USA
LVOW041605191112

308015LV00001B/135/P